This is Kitty Pryde.

She's not happy.

She wants to be a member of the X-Men, but Wolverine won't stop treating her like a kid.

She's going to have to worry about that later, though, because Wolvie's animal nature has been taken away by the HIGH EVOLUTIONARY...

Spotlight   **MARVEL**®

...and Kitty's been turned into a cat!

The LAST KNIGHTS of WUNDAGORE
PART TWO

FRED VAN LENTE   SALVA ESPIN   SOTOMAYOR, QUINTANA, STAPLES   ED DUKESHIRE   DAVIS, FARMER, MOUNTS
WRITER   ARTIST   COLORISTS   LETTERER   COVER

PAUL ACERIOS   NATHAN COSBY   MARK PANICCIA   JOE QUESADA   DAN BUCKLEY
PRODUCTION   ASSISTANT EDITOR   EDITOR   EDITOR IN CHIEF   PUBLISHER

Special Thanks to Guru eFX

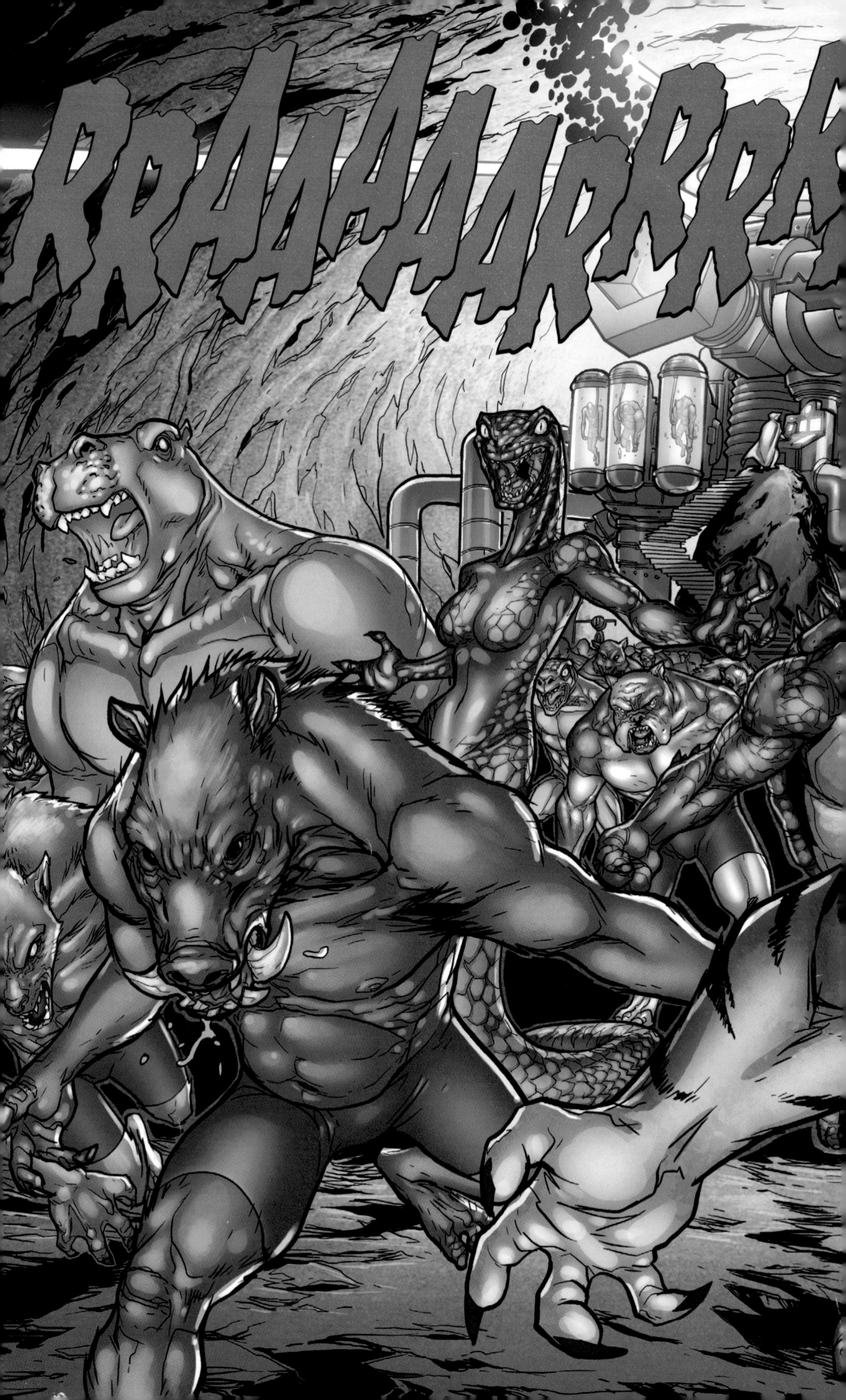
RRAAAAARRR

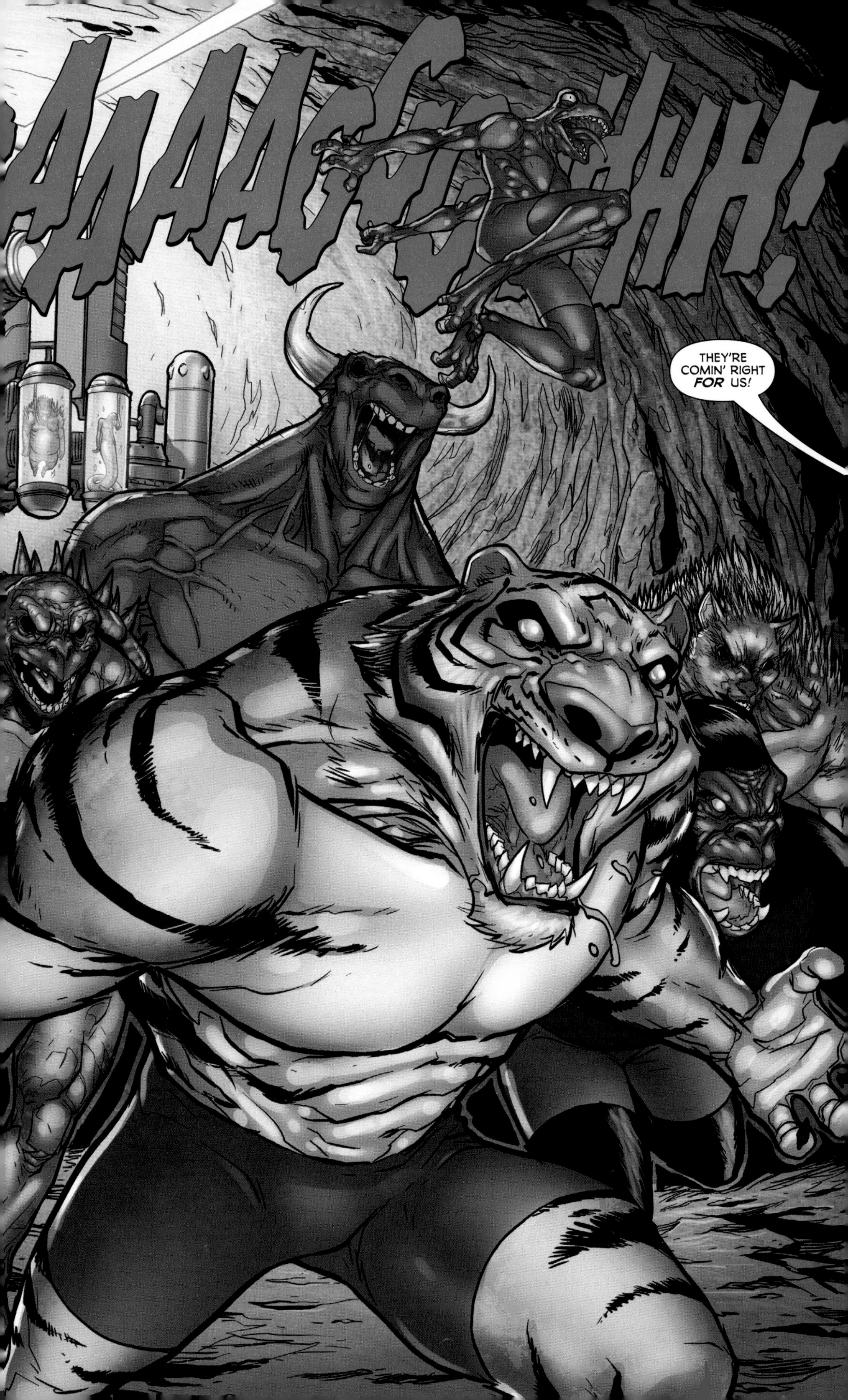
THEY'RE COMIN' RIGHT **FOR** US!

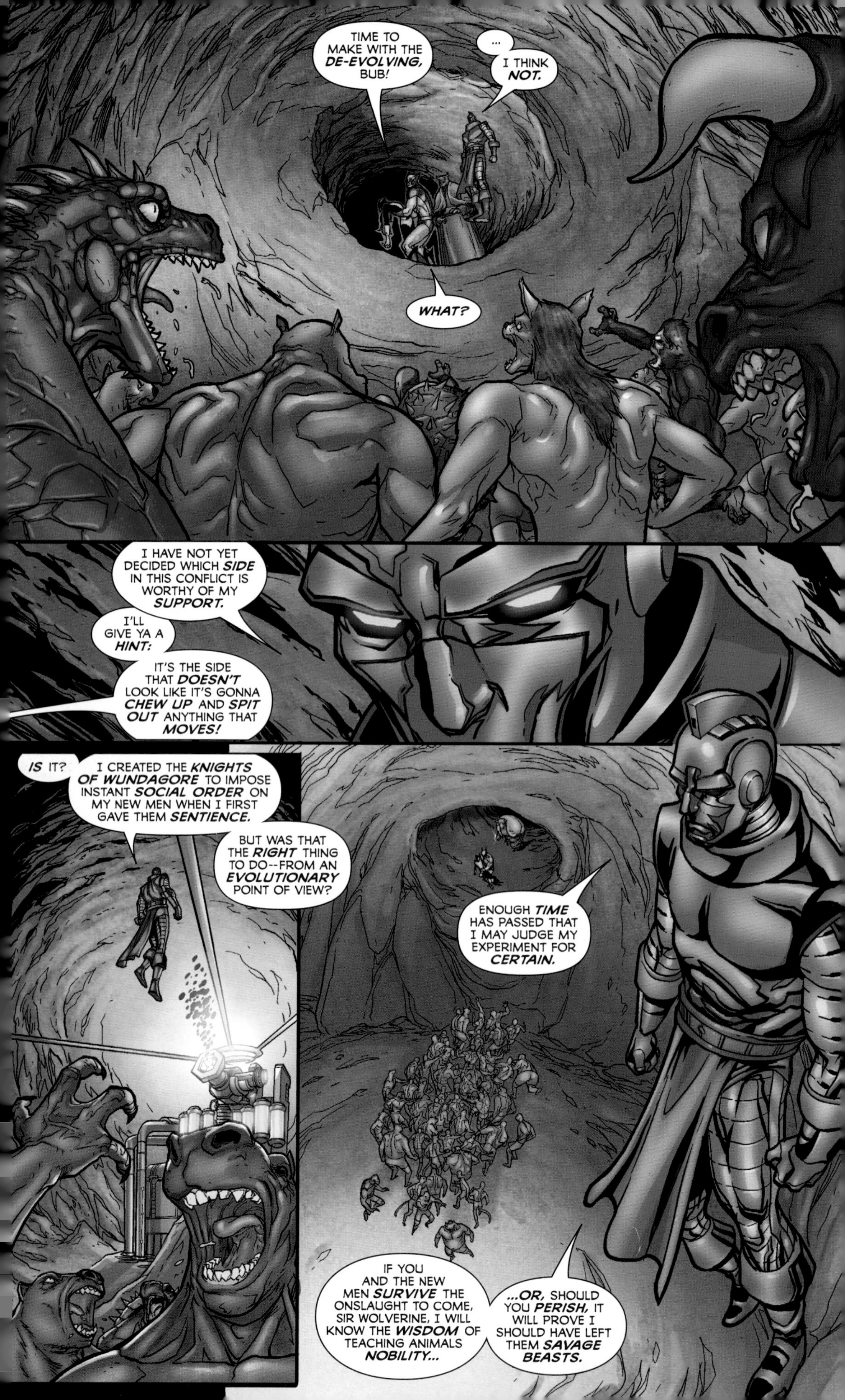
TIME TO MAKE WITH THE DE-EVOLVING, BUB!
... I THINK NOT.
WHAT?
I HAVE NOT YET DECIDED WHICH SIDE IN THIS CONFLICT IS WORTHY OF MY SUPPORT.
I'LL GIVE YA A HINT:
IT'S THE SIDE THAT DOESN'T LOOK LIKE IT'S GONNA CHEW UP AND SPIT OUT ANYTHING THAT MOVES!
IS IT?
I CREATED THE KNIGHTS OF WUNDAGORE TO IMPOSE INSTANT SOCIAL ORDER ON MY NEW MEN WHEN I FIRST GAVE THEM SENTIENCE.
BUT WAS THAT THE RIGHT THING TO DO--FROM AN EVOLUTIONARY POINT OF VIEW?
ENOUGH TIME HAS PASSED THAT I MAY JUDGE MY EXPERIMENT FOR CERTAIN.
IF YOU AND THE NEW MEN SURVIVE THE ONSLAUGHT TO COME, SIR WOLVERINE, I WILL KNOW THE WISDOM OF TEACHING ANIMALS NOBILITY...
...OR, SHOULD YOU PERISH, IT WILL PROVE I SHOULD HAVE LEFT THEM SAVAGE BEASTS.

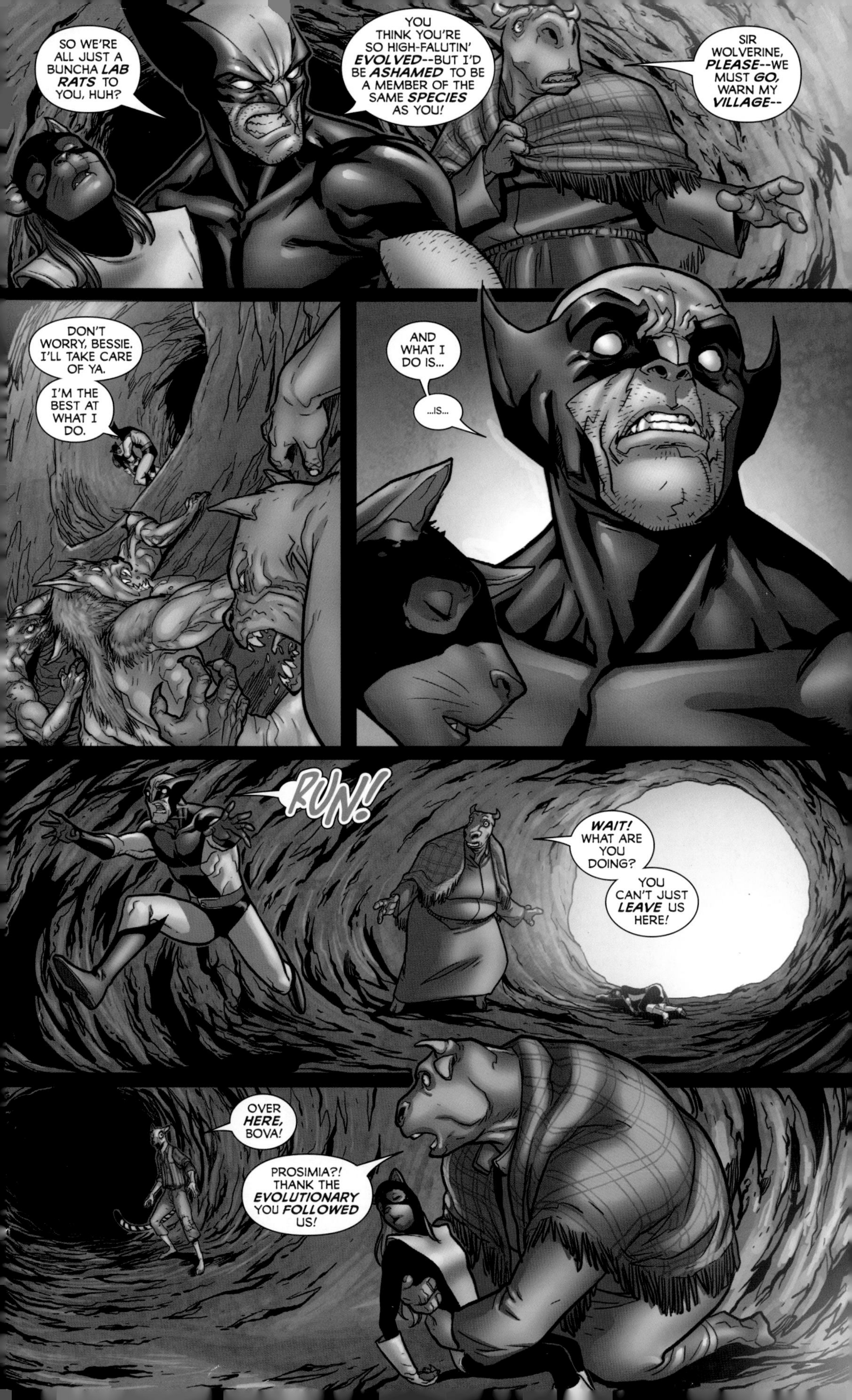
SO WE'RE ALL JUST A BUNCHA LAB RATS TO YOU, HUH?
YOU THINK YOU'RE SO HIGH-FALUTIN' EVOLVED--BUT I'D BE ASHAMED TO BE A MEMBER OF THE SAME SPECIES AS YOU!
SIR WOLVERINE, PLEASE--WE MUST GO, WARN MY VILLAGE--
DON'T WORRY, BESSIE. I'LL TAKE CARE OF YA.
I'M THE BEST AT WHAT I DO.
AND WHAT I DO IS...
...IS...
RUN!
WAIT! WHAT ARE YOU DOING?
YOU CAN'T JUST LEAVE US HERE!
OVER HERE, BOVA!
PROSIMIA?! THANK THE EVOLUTIONARY YOU FOLLOWED US!

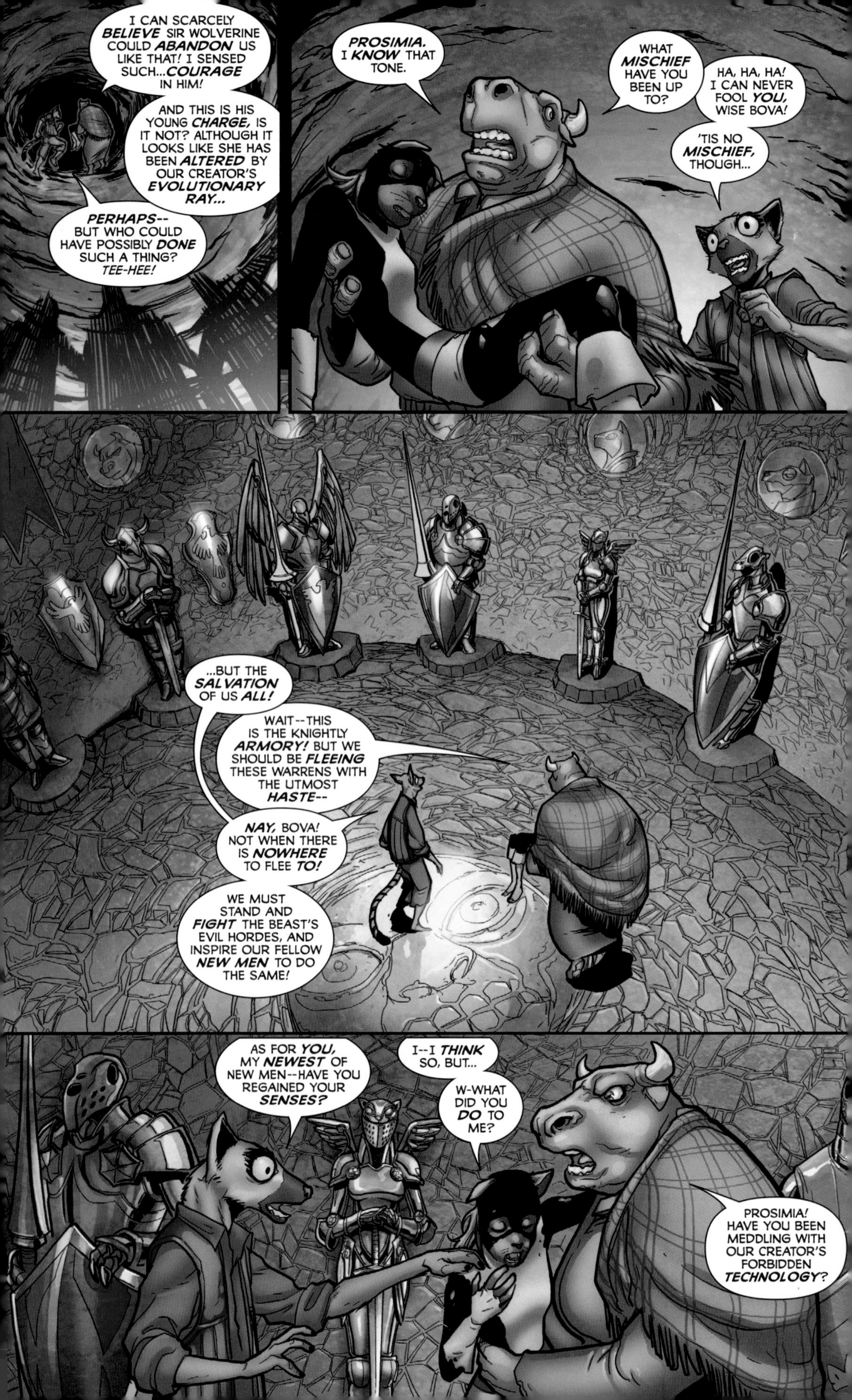
I CAN SCARCELY BELIEVE SIR WOLVERINE COULD ABANDON US LIKE THAT! I SENSED SUCH...COURAGE IN HIM!
AND THIS IS HIS YOUNG CHARGE, IS IT NOT? ALTHOUGH IT LOOKS LIKE SHE HAS BEEN ALTERED BY OUR CREATOR'S EVOLUTIONARY RAY...
PERHAPS-- BUT WHO COULD HAVE POSSIBLY DONE SUCH A THING? TEE-HEE!
PROSIMIA. I KNOW THAT TONE.
WHAT MISCHIEF HAVE YOU BEEN UP TO?
HA, HA, HA! I CAN NEVER FOOL YOU, WISE BOVA!
'TIS NO MISCHIEF, THOUGH...
...BUT THE SALVATION OF US ALL!
WAIT--THIS IS THE KNIGHTLY ARMORY! BUT WE SHOULD BE FLEEING THESE WARRENS WITH THE UTMOST HASTE--
NAY, BOVA! NOT WHEN THERE IS NOWHERE TO FLEE TO!
WE MUST STAND AND FIGHT THE BEAST'S EVIL HORDES, AND INSPIRE OUR FELLOW NEW MEN TO DO THE SAME!
AS FOR YOU, MY NEWEST OF NEW MEN--HAVE YOU REGAINED YOUR SENSES?
I--I THINK SO, BUT...
W-WHAT DID YOU DO TO ME?
PROSIMIA! HAVE YOU BEEN MEDDLING WITH OUR CREATOR'S FORBIDDEN TECHNOLOGY?

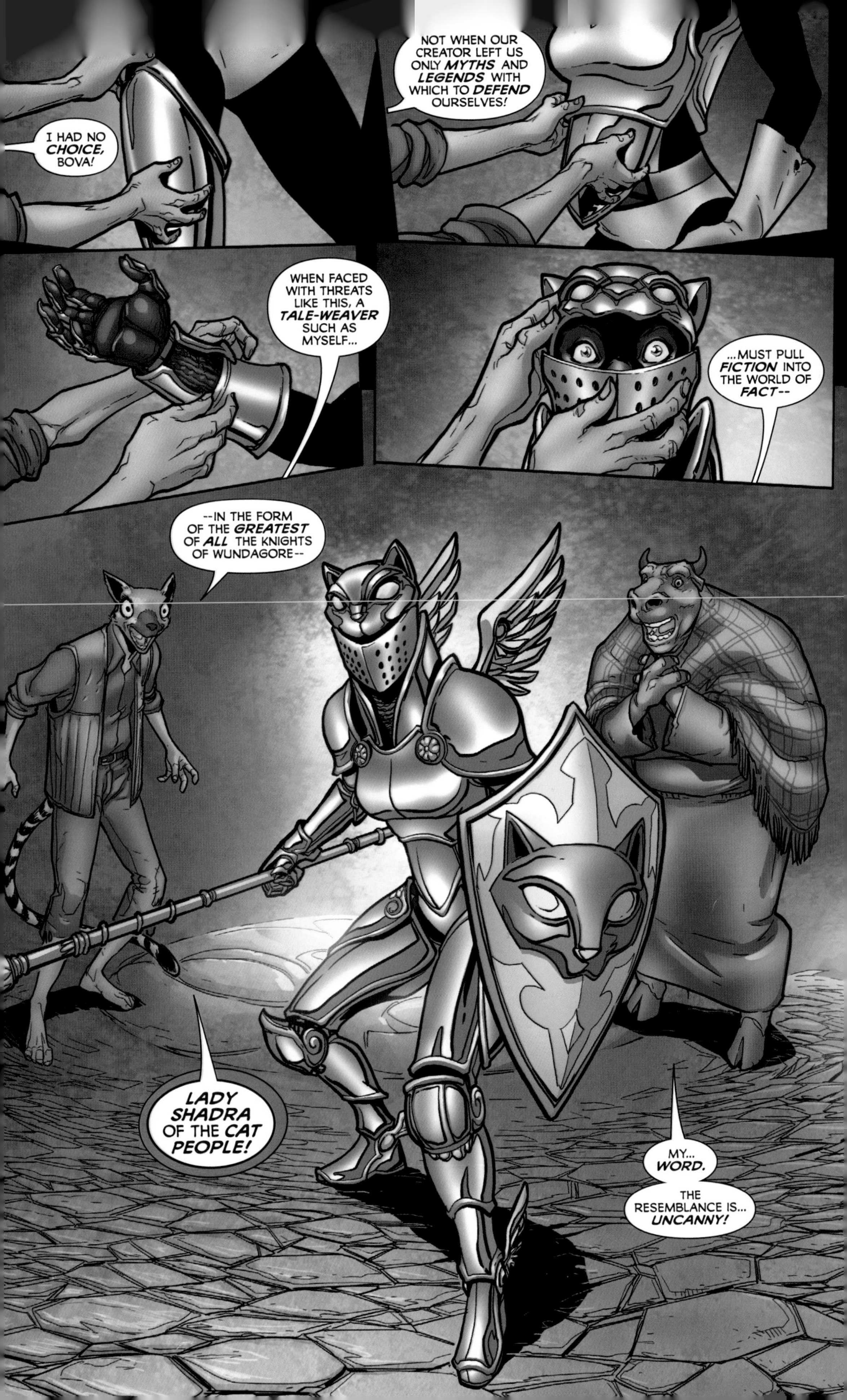

I HAD NO CHOICE, BOVA!
NOT WHEN OUR CREATOR LEFT US ONLY MYTHS AND LEGENDS WITH WHICH TO DEFEND OURSELVES!
WHEN FACED WITH THREATS LIKE THIS, A TALE-WEAVER SUCH AS MYSELF...
...MUST PULL FICTION INTO THE WORLD OF FACT--
--IN THE FORM OF THE GREATEST OF ALL THE KNIGHTS OF WUNDAGORE--
LADY SHADRA OF THE CAT PEOPLE!
MY... WORD.
THE RESEMBLANCE IS... UNCANNY!

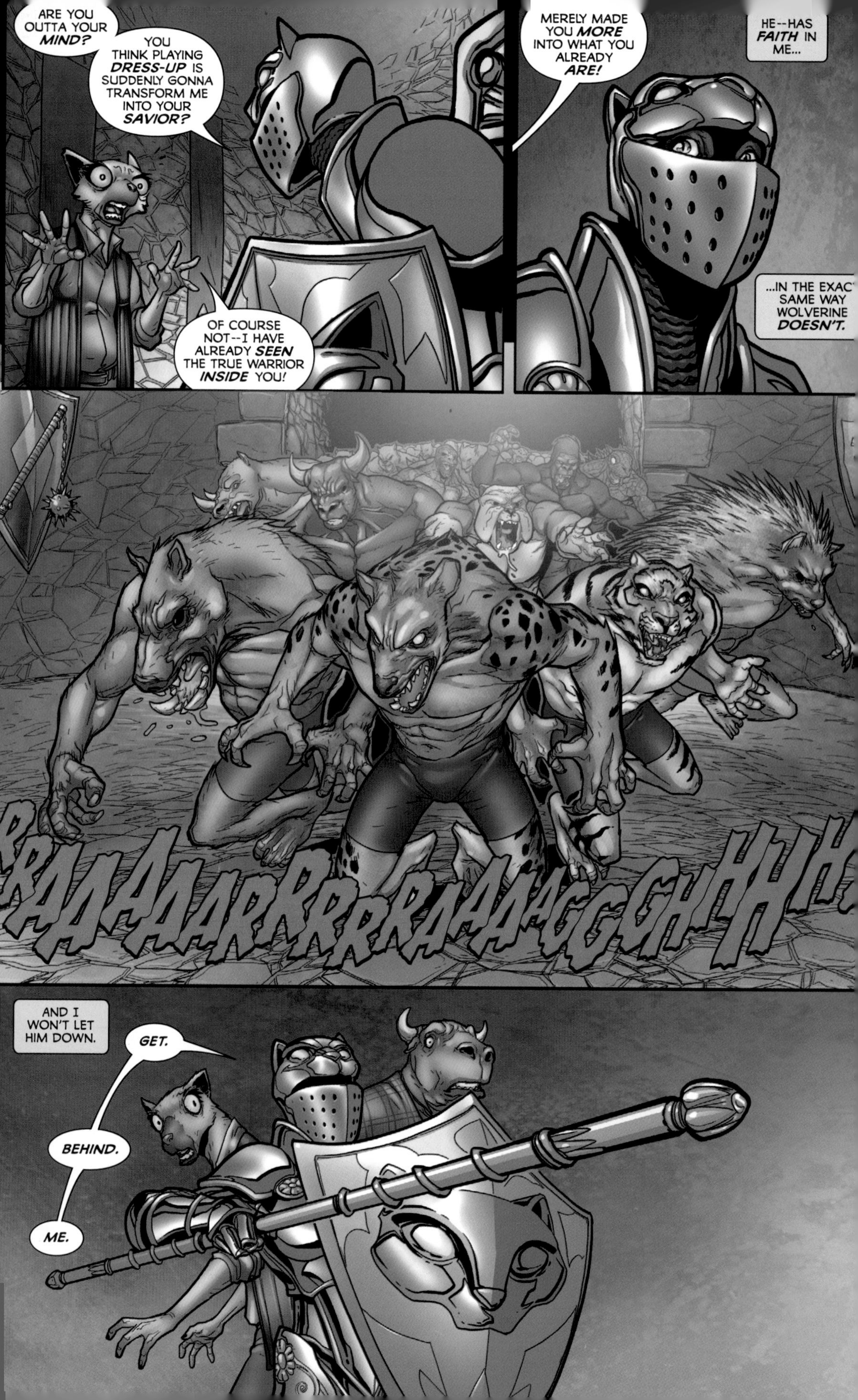
ARE YOU OUTTA YOUR MIND?
YOU THINK PLAYING DRESS-UP IS SUDDENLY GONNA TRANSFORM ME INTO YOUR SAVIOR?
OF COURSE NOT--I HAVE ALREADY SEEN THE TRUE WARRIOR INSIDE YOU!
MERELY MADE YOU MORE INTO WHAT YOU ALREADY ARE!
HE--HAS FAITH IN ME...
...IN THE EXAC SAME WAY WOLVERINE DOESN'T.
RAAAAAARRRRRAAAAGGGHHHH
AND I WON'T LET HIM DOWN.
GET.
BEHIND.
ME.

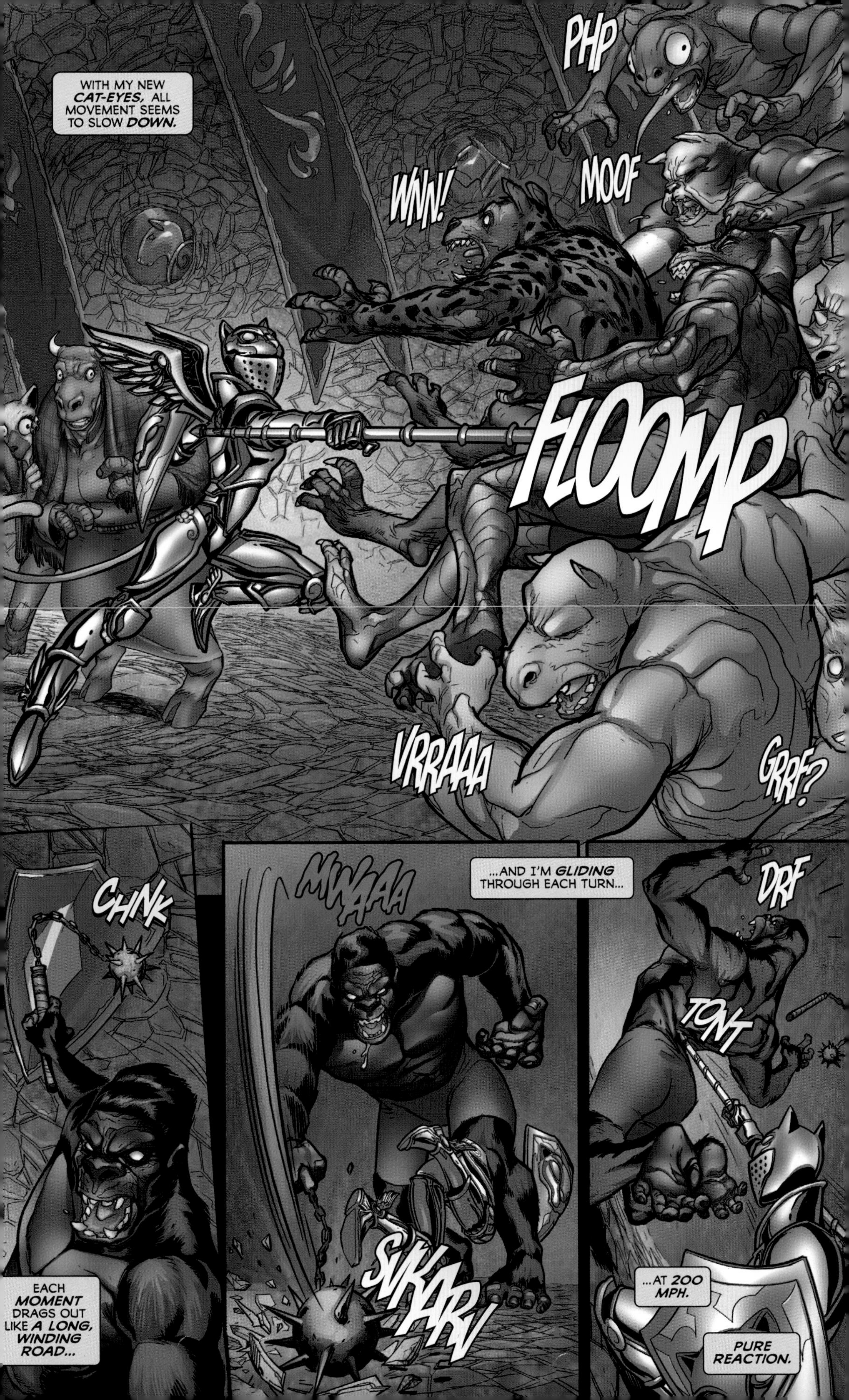

WITH MY NEW *CAT-EYES,* ALL MOVEMENT SEEMS TO SLOW *DOWN.*
PHP
WNN!
MOOF
FLOOMP
VRRAAA
GRRF?
CHINK
EACH *MOMENT* DRAGS OUT LIKE *A LONG, WINDING ROAD...*
MWAAA
...AND I'M *GLIDING* THROUGH EACH TURN...
SKARV
DRF
TONT
...AT *200 MPH.*
PURE REACTION.

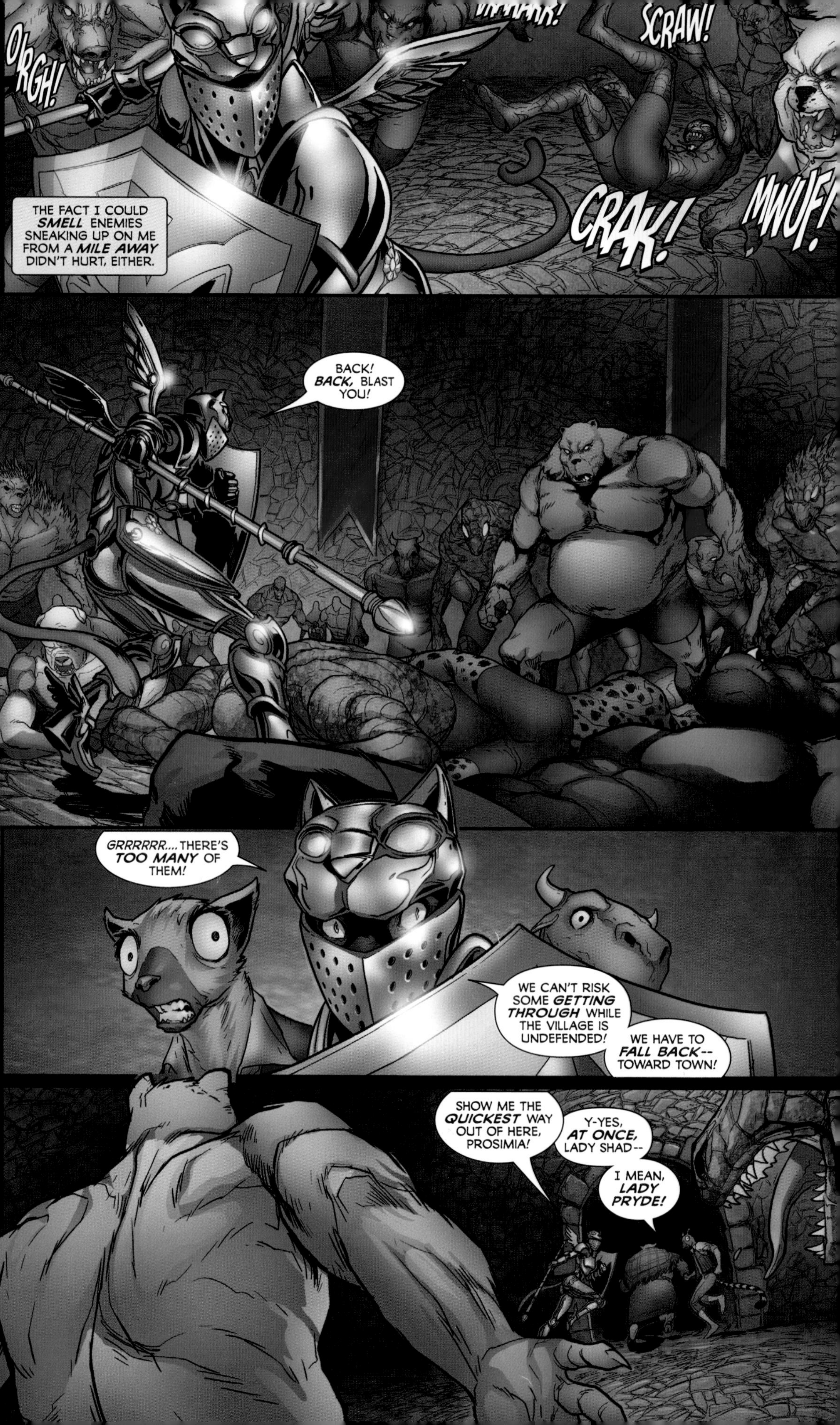

ORGH!
SCRAW!
THE FACT I COULD SMELL ENEMIES SNEAKING UP ON ME FROM A MILE AWAY DIDN'T HURT, EITHER.
CRAK!
MWUF!
BACK! BACK, BLAST YOU!
GRRRRRR.... THERE'S TOO MANY OF THEM!
WE CAN'T RISK SOME GETTING THROUGH WHILE THE VILLAGE IS UNDEFENDED!
WE HAVE TO FALL BACK-- TOWARD TOWN!
SHOW ME THE QUICKEST WAY OUT OF HERE, PROSIMIA!
Y-YES, AT ONCE, LADY SHAD--
I MEAN, LADY PRYDE!

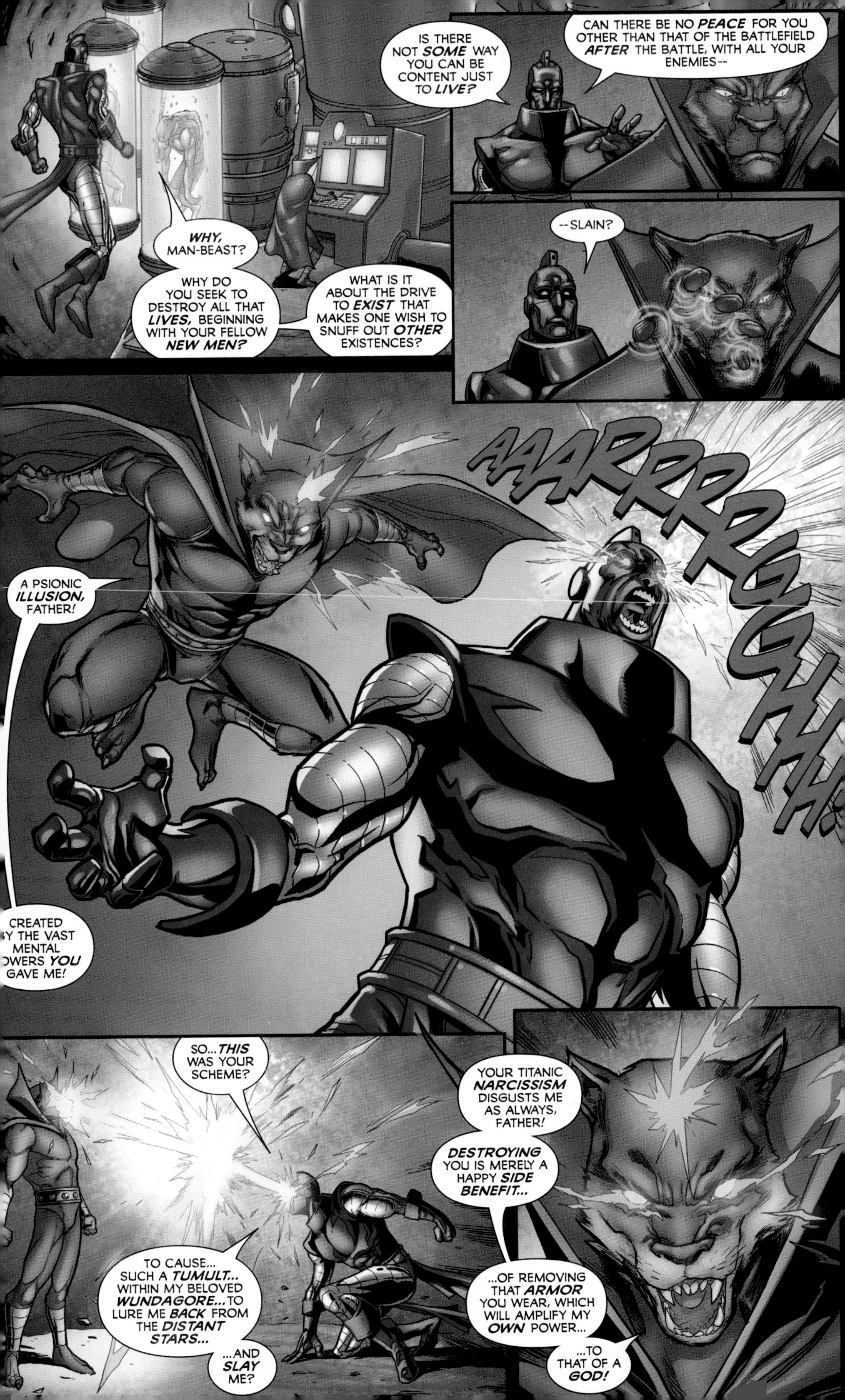

WHY, MAN-BEAST?
WHY DO YOU SEEK TO DESTROY ALL THAT LIVES, BEGINNING WITH YOUR FELLOW NEW MEN?
WHAT IS IT ABOUT THE DRIVE TO EXIST THAT MAKES ONE WISH TO SNUFF OUT OTHER EXISTENCES?
IS THERE NOT SOME WAY YOU CAN BE CONTENT JUST TO LIVE?
CAN THERE BE NO PEACE FOR YOU OTHER THAN THAT OF THE BATTLEFIELD AFTER THE BATTLE, WITH ALL YOUR ENEMIES--
--SLAIN?
AAARRRRGHH!
A PSIONIC ILLUSION, FATHER!
CREATED BY THE VAST MENTAL POWERS YOU GAVE ME!
SO...THIS WAS YOUR SCHEME?
TO CAUSE... SUCH A TUMULT... WITHIN MY BELOVED WUNDAGORE...TO LURE ME BACK FROM THE DISTANT STARS...
...AND SLAY ME?
YOUR TITANIC NARCISSISM DISGUSTS ME AS ALWAYS, FATHER!
DESTROYING YOU IS MERELY A HAPPY SIDE BENEFIT...
...OF REMOVING THAT ARMOR YOU WEAR, WHICH WILL AMPLIFY MY OWN POWER...
...TO THAT OF A GOD!

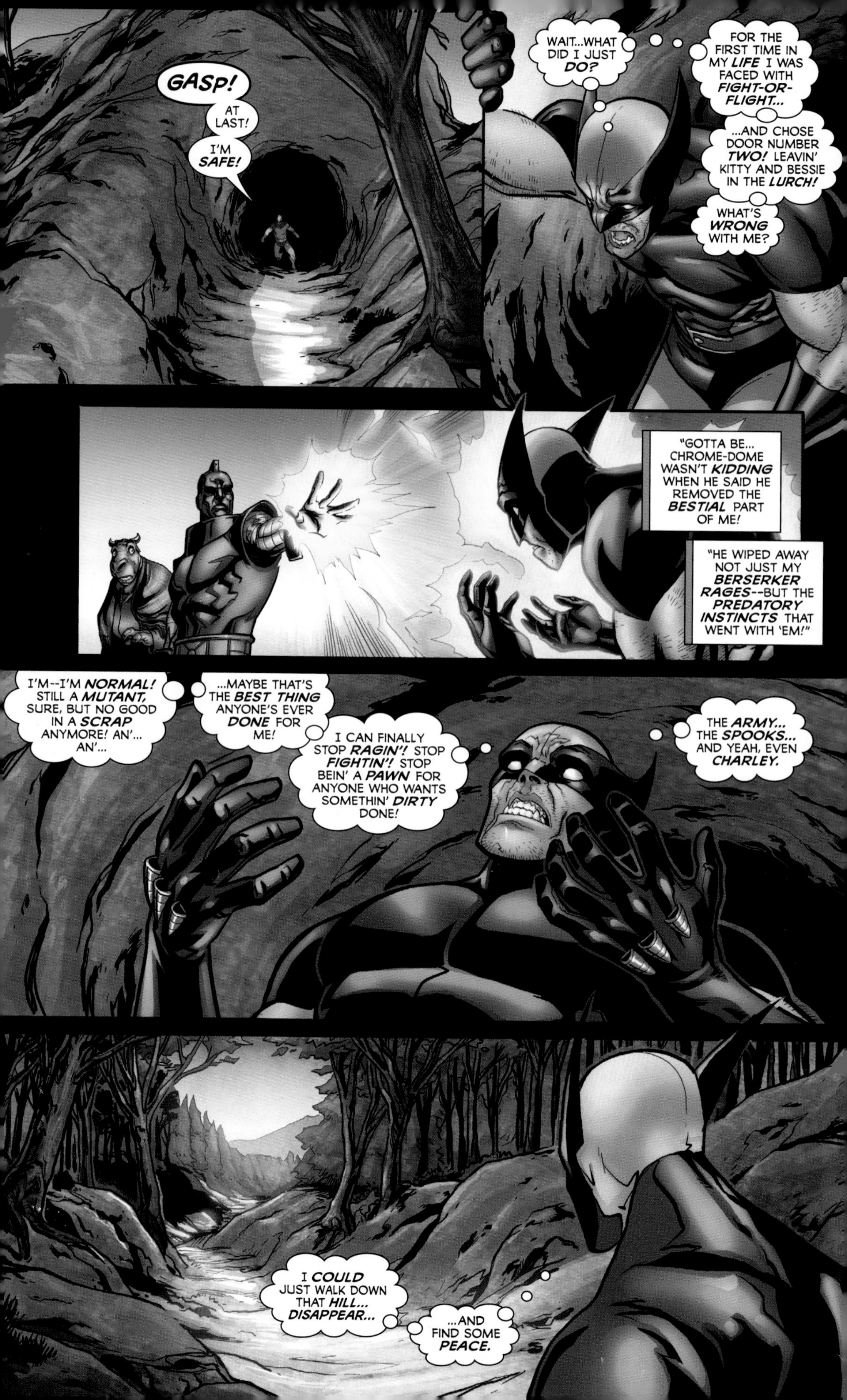
GASP!
AT LAST!
I'M SAFE!
WAIT...WHAT DID I JUST DO?
FOR THE FIRST TIME IN MY LIFE I WAS FACED WITH FIGHT-OR-FLIGHT...
...AND CHOSE DOOR NUMBER TWO! LEAVIN' KITTY AND BESSIE IN THE LURCH!
WHAT'S WRONG WITH ME?
"GOTTA BE... CHROME-DOME WASN'T KIDDING WHEN HE SAID HE REMOVED THE BESTIAL PART OF ME!
"HE WIPED AWAY NOT JUST MY BERSERKER RAGES--BUT THE PREDATORY INSTINCTS THAT WENT WITH 'EM!"
I'M--I'M NORMAL! STILL A MUTANT, SURE, BUT NO GOOD IN A SCRAP ANYMORE! AN'... AN'...
...MAYBE THAT'S THE BEST THING ANYONE'S EVER DONE FOR ME!
I CAN FINALLY STOP RAGIN'! STOP FIGHTIN'! STOP BEIN' A PAWN FOR ANYONE WHO WANTS SOMETHIN' DIRTY DONE!
THE ARMY... THE SPOOKS... AND YEAH, EVEN CHARLEY.
I COULD JUST WALK DOWN THAT HILL... DISAPPEAR...
...AND FIND SOME PEACE.

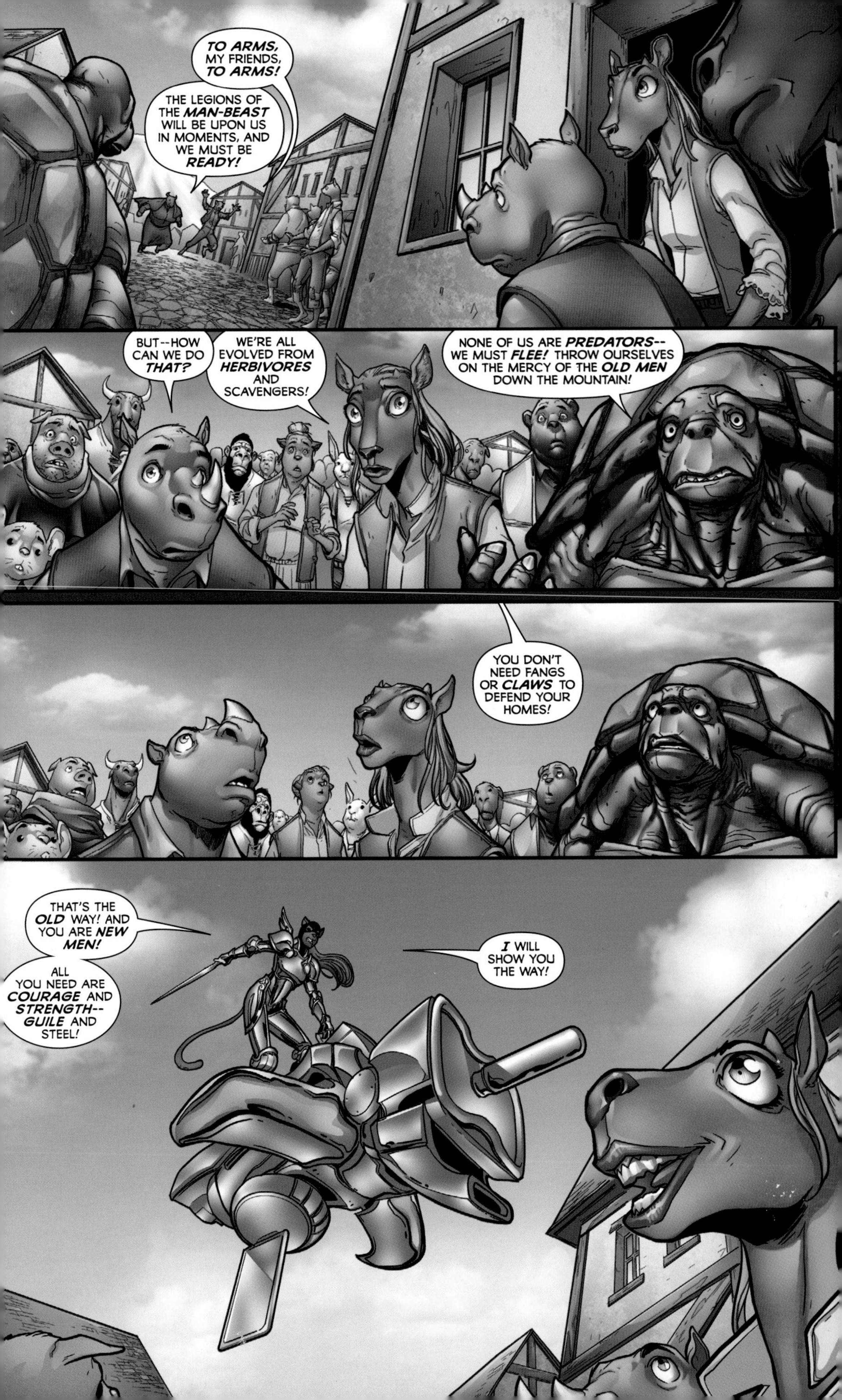
TO ARMS, MY FRIENDS, TO ARMS!
THE LEGIONS OF THE MAN-BEAST WILL BE UPON US IN MOMENTS, AND WE MUST BE READY!
BUT--HOW CAN WE DO THAT?
WE'RE ALL EVOLVED FROM HERBIVORES AND SCAVENGERS!
NONE OF US ARE PREDATORS-- WE MUST FLEE! THROW OURSELVES ON THE MERCY OF THE OLD MEN DOWN THE MOUNTAIN!
YOU DON'T NEED FANGS OR CLAWS TO DEFEND YOUR HOMES!
THAT'S THE OLD WAY! AND YOU ARE NEW MEN!
ALL YOU NEED ARE COURAGE AND STRENGTH-- GUILE AND STEEL!
I WILL SHOW YOU THE WAY!

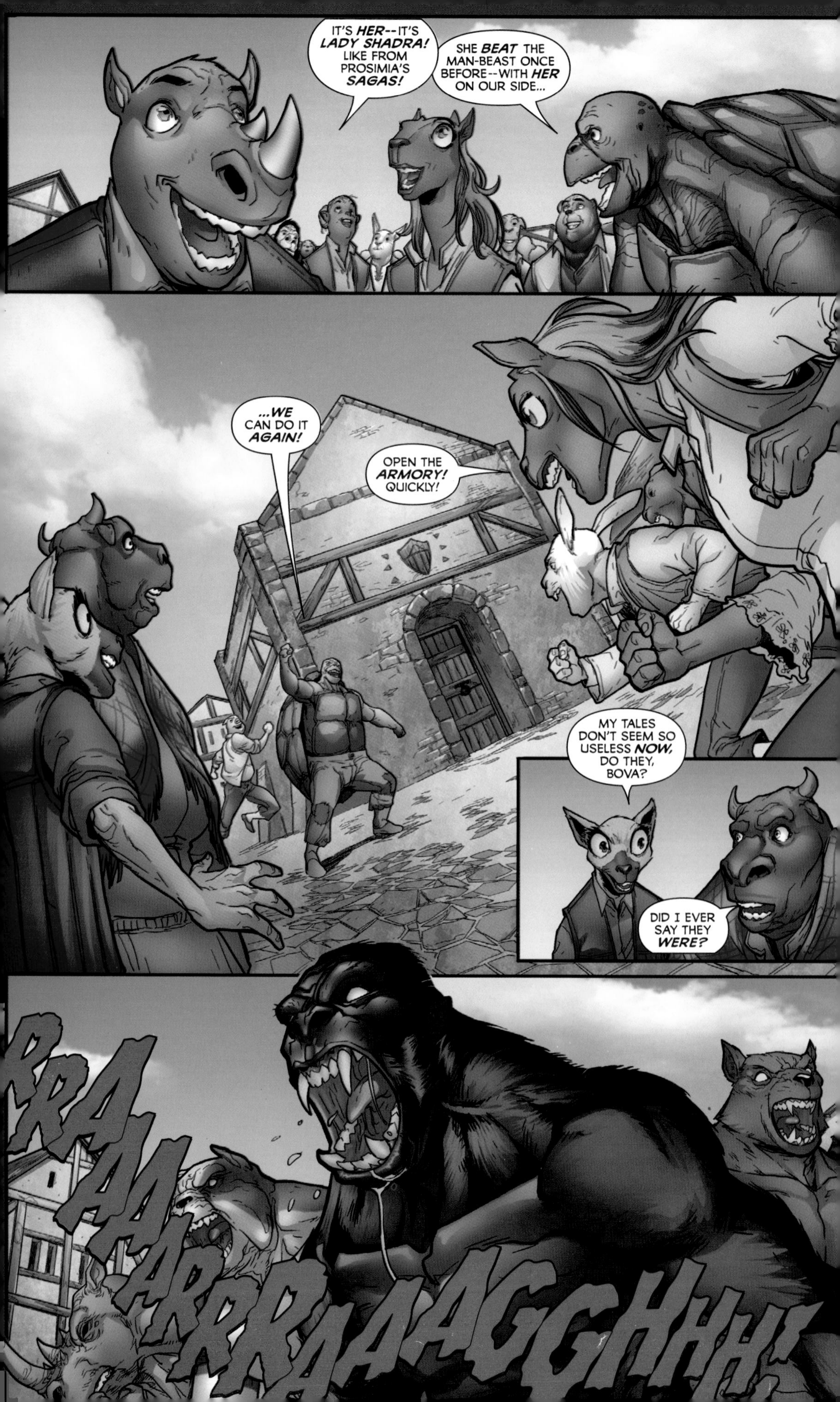

IT'S HER--IT'S LADY SHADRA! LIKE FROM PROSIMIA'S SAGAS!
SHE BEAT THE MAN-BEAST ONCE BEFORE--WITH HER ON OUR SIDE...
...WE CAN DO IT AGAIN!
OPEN THE ARMORY! QUICKLY!
MY TALES DON'T SEEM SO USELESS NOW, DO THEY, BOVA?
DID I EVER SAY THEY WERE?
RRAAARRRAAAGGHHH!

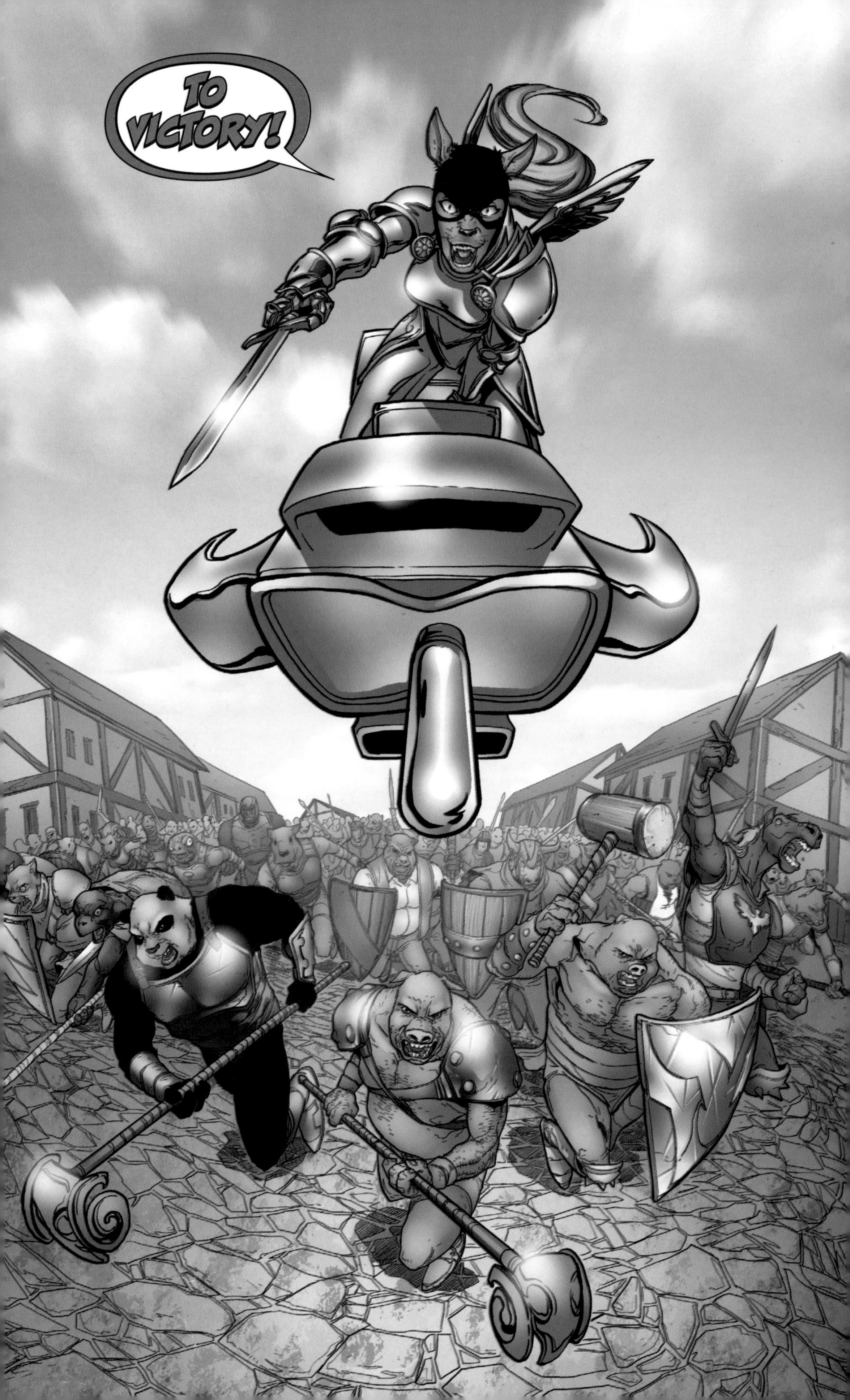
TO VICTORY!

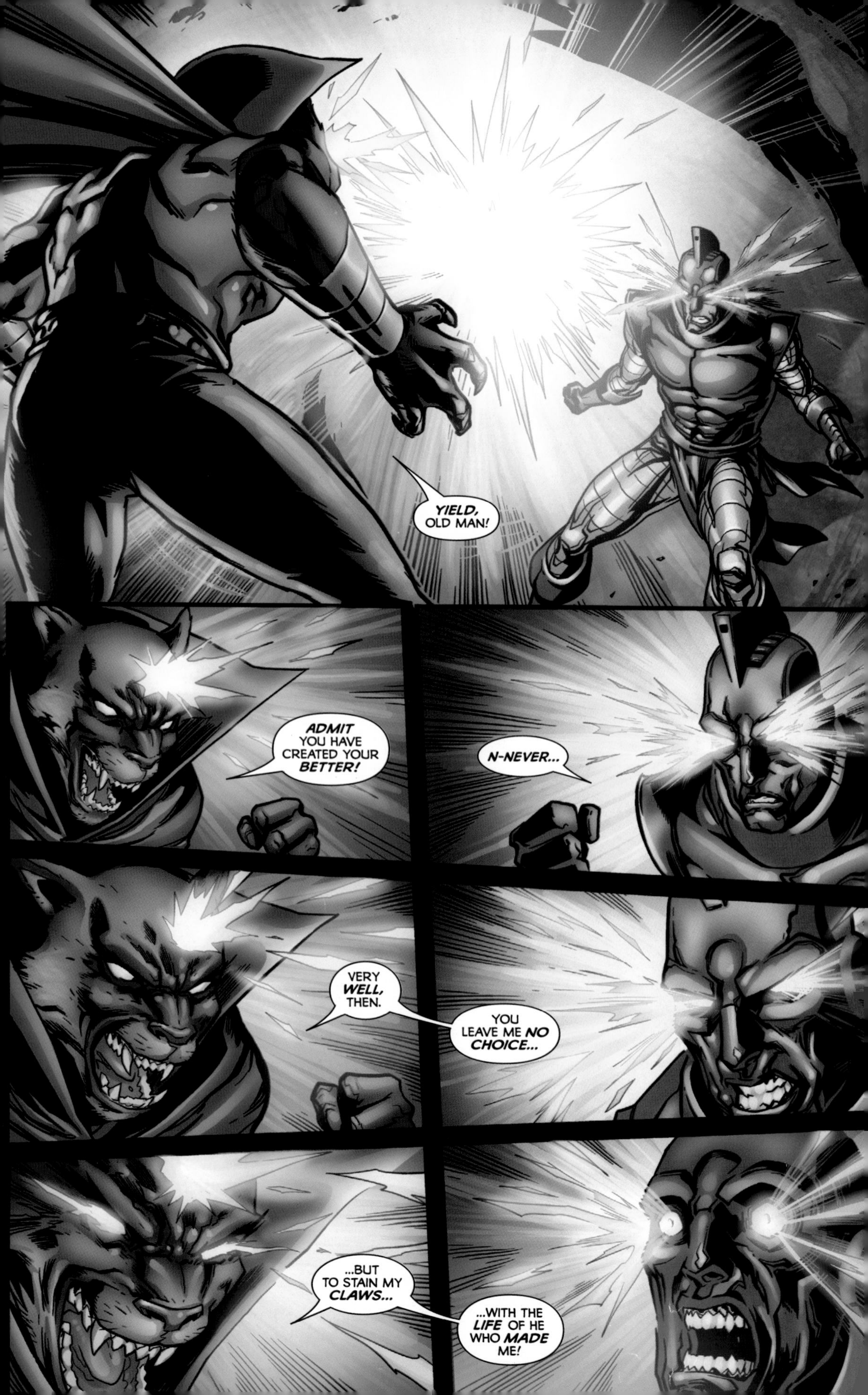
YIELD, OLD MAN!
ADMIT YOU HAVE CREATED YOUR BETTER!
N-NEVER...
VERY WELL, THEN.
YOU LEAVE ME NO CHOICE...
...BUT TO STAIN MY CLAWS...
...WITH THE LIFE OF HE WHO MADE ME!

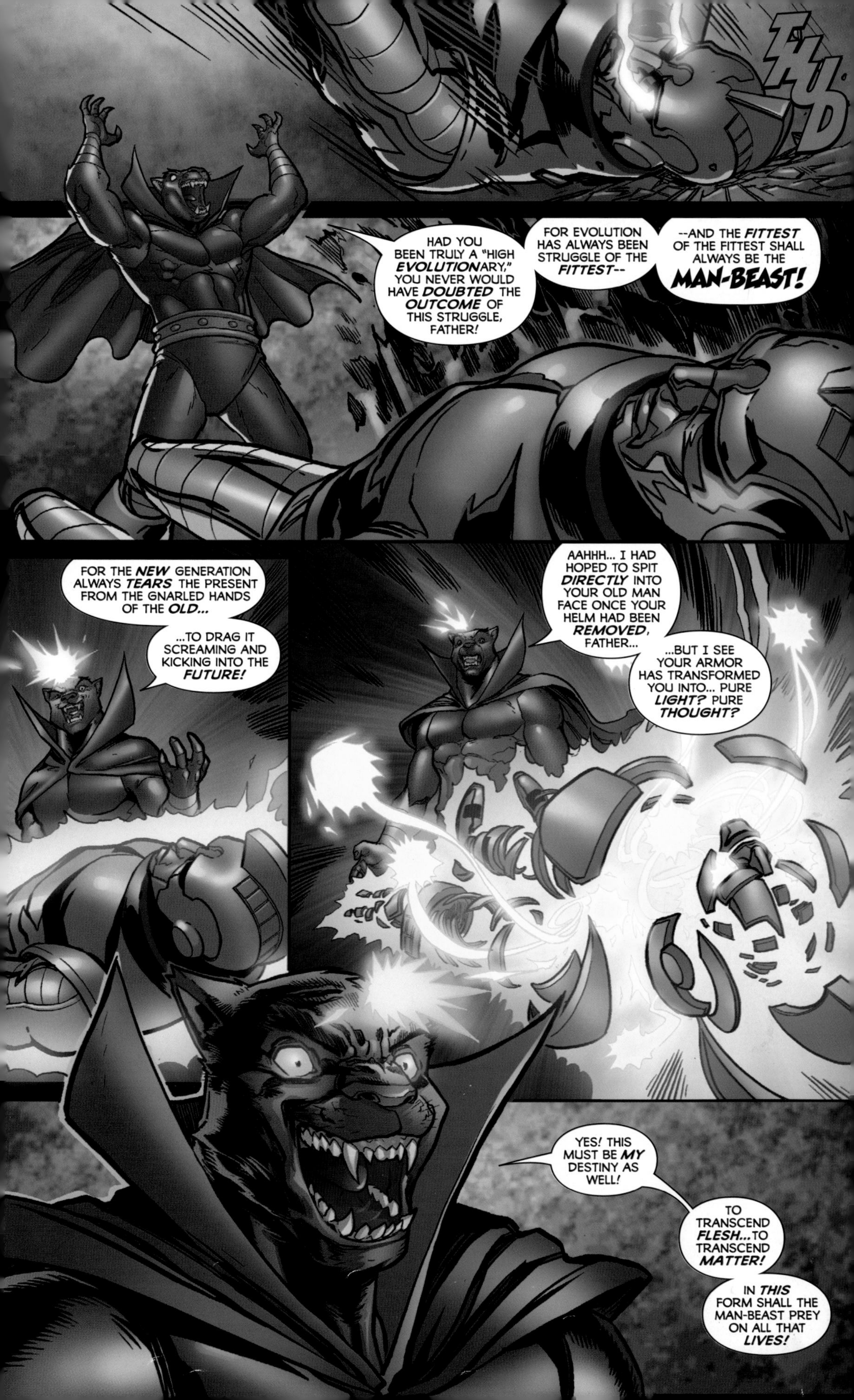
THUD
HAD YOU BEEN TRULY A "HIGH EVOLUTIONARY," YOU NEVER WOULD HAVE DOUBTED THE OUTCOME OF THIS STRUGGLE, FATHER!
FOR EVOLUTION HAS ALWAYS BEEN STRUGGLE OF THE FITTEST--
--AND THE FITTEST OF THE FITTEST SHALL ALWAYS BE THE MAN-BEAST!
FOR THE NEW GENERATION ALWAYS TEARS THE PRESENT FROM THE GNARLED HANDS OF THE OLD...
...TO DRAG IT SCREAMING AND KICKING INTO THE FUTURE!
AAHHH... I HAD HOPED TO SPIT DIRECTLY INTO YOUR OLD MAN FACE ONCE YOUR HELM HAD BEEN REMOVED, FATHER...
...BUT I SEE YOUR ARMOR HAS TRANSFORMED YOU INTO... PURE LIGHT? PURE THOUGHT?
YES! THIS MUST BE MY DESTINY AS WELL!
TO TRANSCEND FLESH... TO TRANSCEND MATTER!
IN THIS FORM SHALL THE MAN-BEAST PREY ON ALL THAT LIVES!

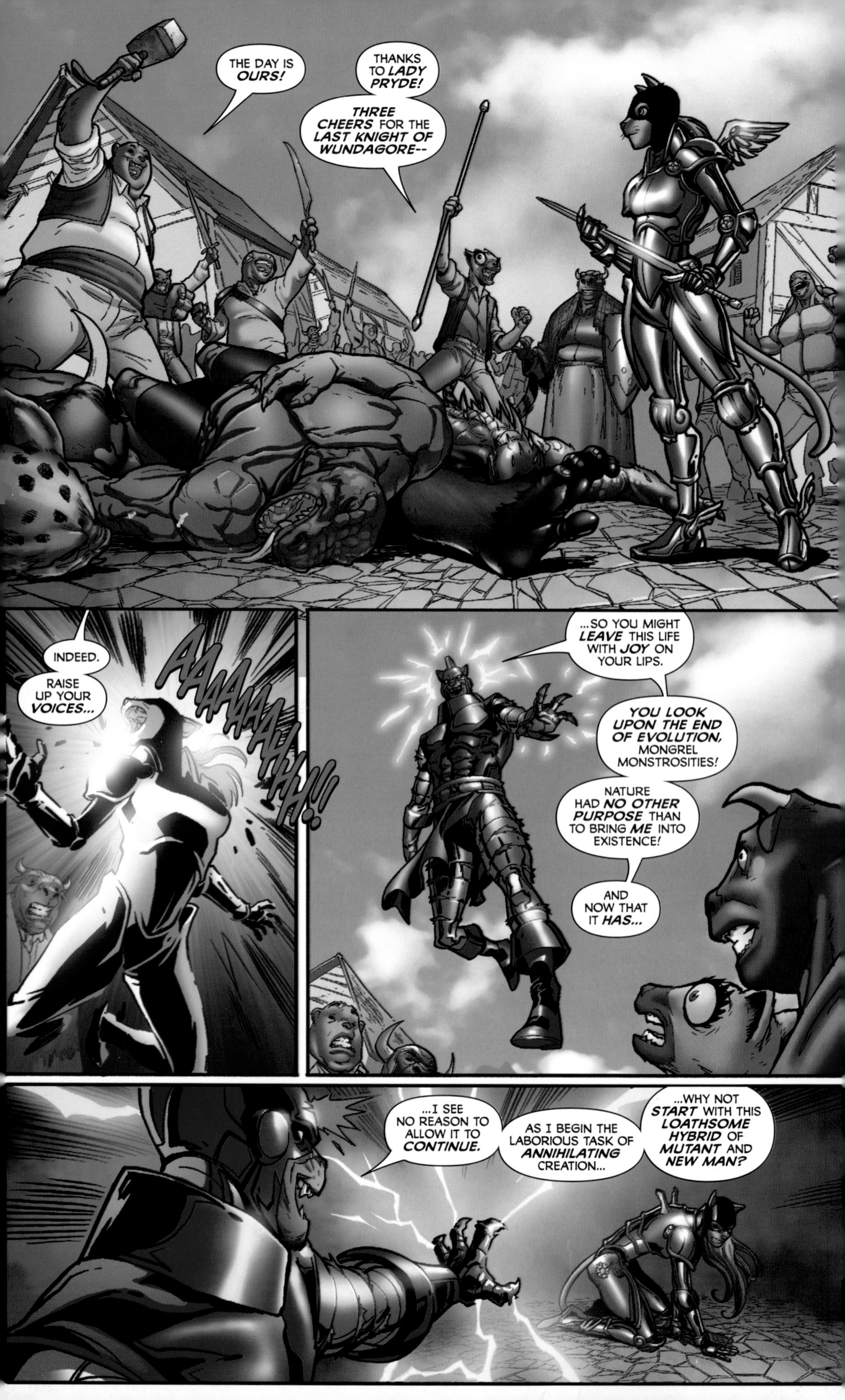
THE DAY IS OURS!
THANKS TO LADY PRYDE!
THREE CHEERS FOR THE LAST KNIGHT OF WUNDAGORE--
INDEED.
RAISE UP YOUR VOICES...
AAAAAAAAAHHH!!!
...SO YOU MIGHT LEAVE THIS LIFE WITH JOY ON YOUR LIPS.
YOU LOOK UPON THE END OF EVOLUTION, MONGREL MONSTROSITIES!
NATURE HAD NO OTHER PURPOSE THAN TO BRING ME INTO EXISTENCE!
AND NOW THAT IT HAS...
...I SEE NO REASON TO ALLOW IT TO CONTINUE.
AS I BEGIN THE LABORIOUS TASK OF ANNIHILATING CREATION...
...WHY NOT START WITH THIS LOATHSOME HYBRID OF MUTANT AND NEW MAN?

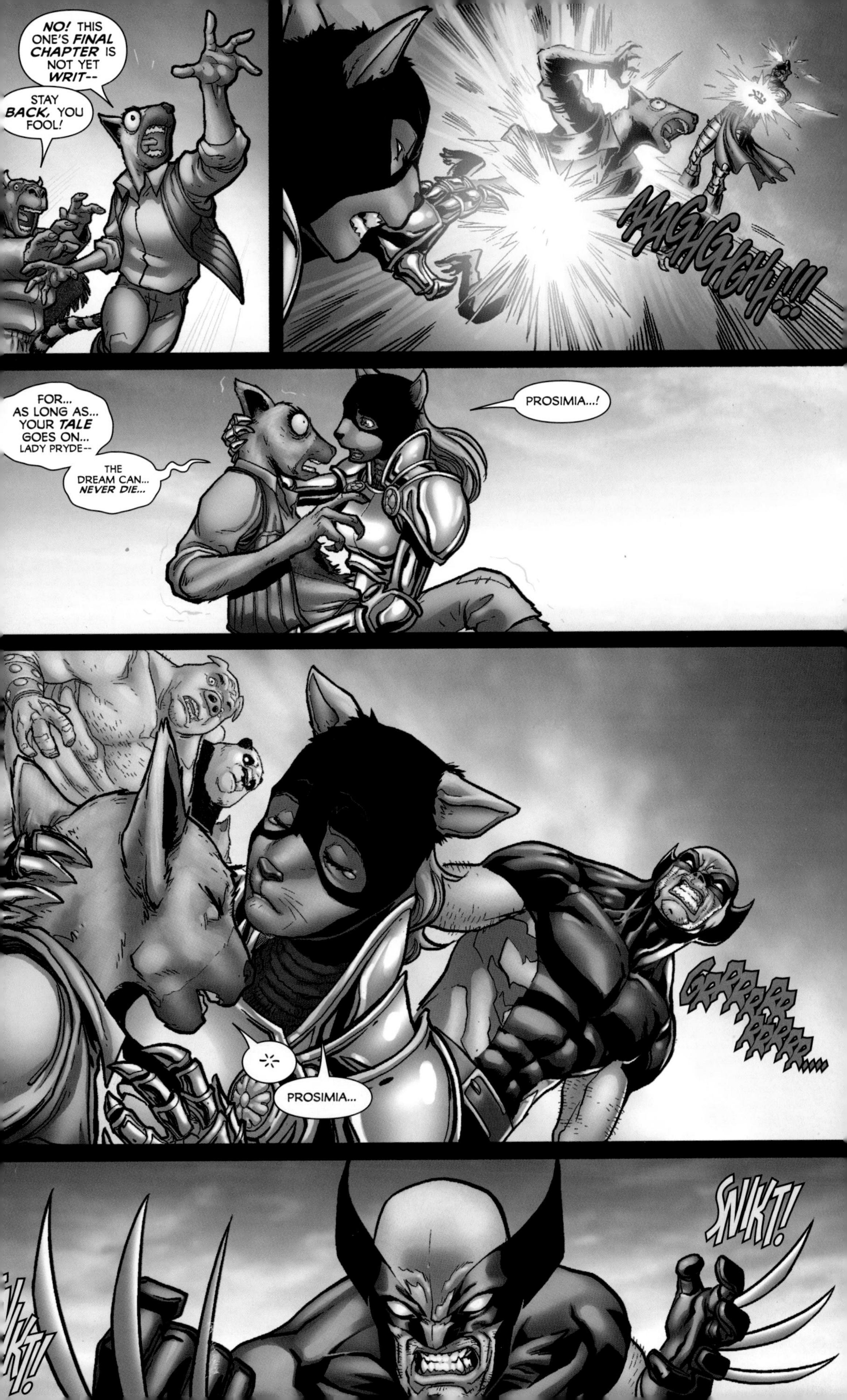
NO! THIS ONE'S FINAL CHAPTER IS NOT YET WRIT--
STAY BACK, YOU FOOL!
AAAGHGHGHH!!!..
FOR... AS LONG AS... YOUR TALE GOES ON... LADY PRYDE--
THE DREAM CAN... NEVER DIE...
PROSIMIA...!
PROSIMIA...
GRRRRRR RRRRR.....
SNIKT!
SNIKT!

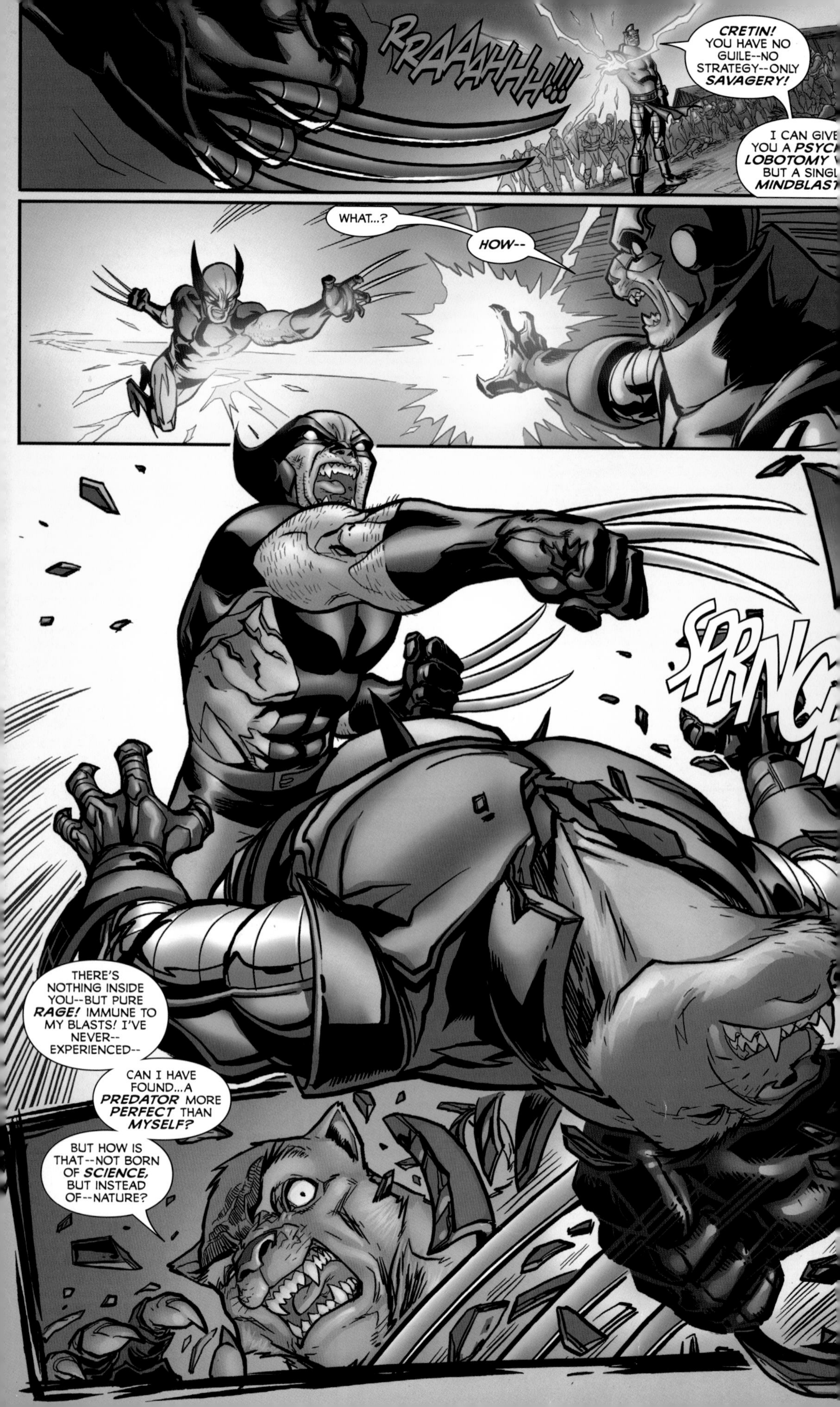
RRAAAHHH!!!
CRETIN! YOU HAVE NO GUILE--NO STRATEGY--ONLY SAVAGERY!
I CAN GIVE YOU A PSYC LOBOTOMY BUT A SINGL MINDBLAST
WHAT...?
HOW--
SPRNCH
THERE'S NOTHING INSIDE YOU--BUT PURE RAGE! IMMUNE TO MY BLASTS! I'VE NEVER-- EXPERIENCED--
CAN I HAVE FOUND...A PREDATOR MORE PERFECT THAN MYSELF?
BUT HOW IS THAT--NOT BORN OF SCIENCE, BUT INSTEAD OF--NATURE?

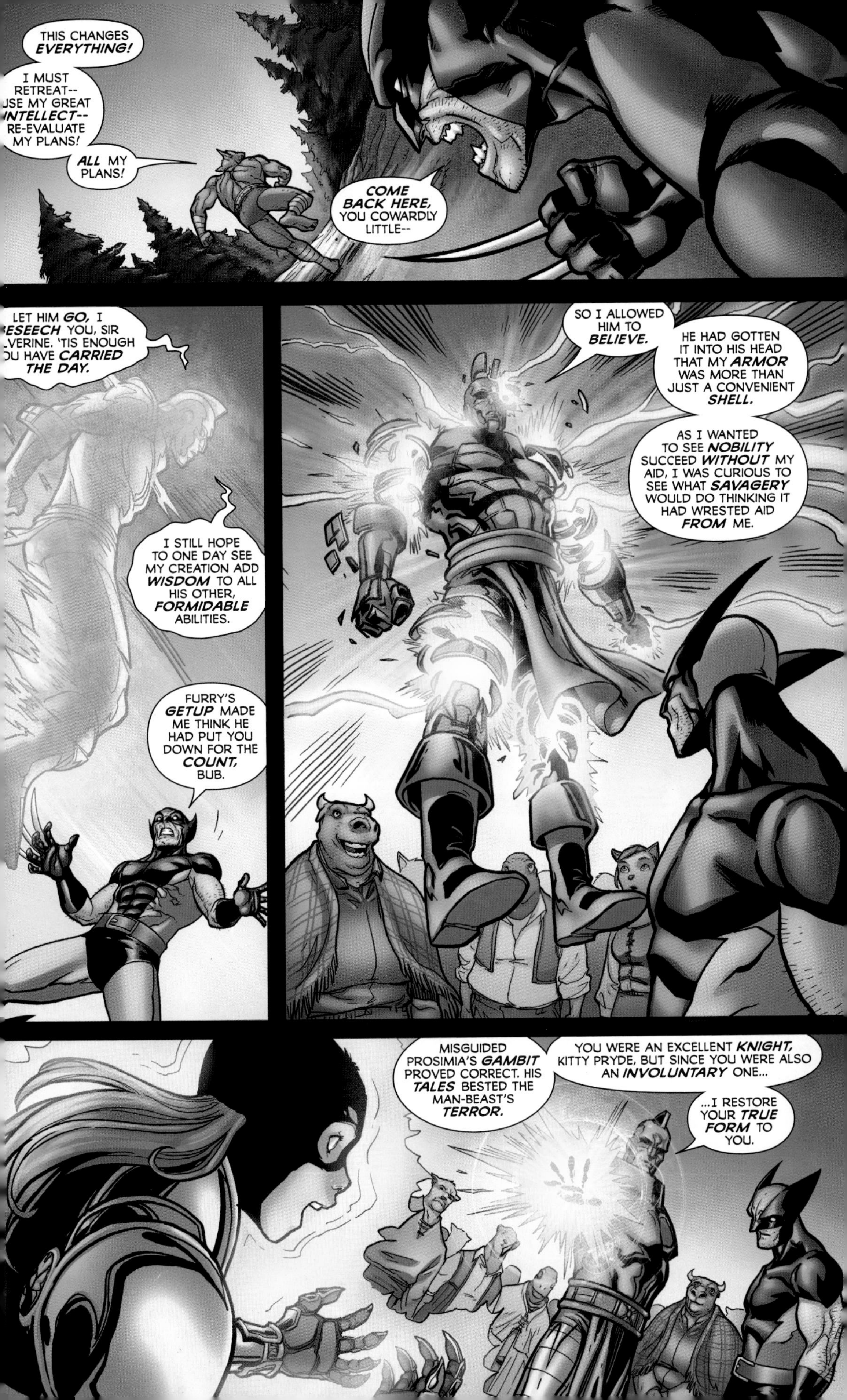
THIS CHANGES EVERYTHING!
I MUST RETREAT-- USE MY GREAT INTELLECT-- RE-EVALUATE MY PLANS!
ALL MY PLANS!
COME BACK HERE, YOU COWARDLY LITTLE--
LET HIM GO, I BESEECH YOU, SIR WOLVERINE. 'TIS ENOUGH YOU HAVE CARRIED THE DAY.
I STILL HOPE TO ONE DAY SEE MY CREATION ADD WISDOM TO ALL HIS OTHER, FORMIDABLE ABILITIES.
FURRY'S GETUP MADE ME THINK HE HAD PUT YOU DOWN FOR THE COUNT, BUB.
SO I ALLOWED HIM TO BELIEVE.
HE HAD GOTTEN IT INTO HIS HEAD THAT MY ARMOR WAS MORE THAN JUST A CONVENIENT SHELL.
AS I WANTED TO SEE NOBILITY SUCCEED WITHOUT MY AID, I WAS CURIOUS TO SEE WHAT SAVAGERY WOULD DO THINKING IT HAD WRESTED AID FROM ME.
MISGUIDED PROSIMIA'S GAMBIT PROVED CORRECT. HIS TALES BESTED THE MAN-BEAST'S TERROR.
YOU WERE AN EXCELLENT KNIGHT, KITTY PRYDE, BUT SINCE YOU WERE ALSO AN INVOLUNTARY ONE...
...I RESTORE YOUR TRUE FORM TO YOU.

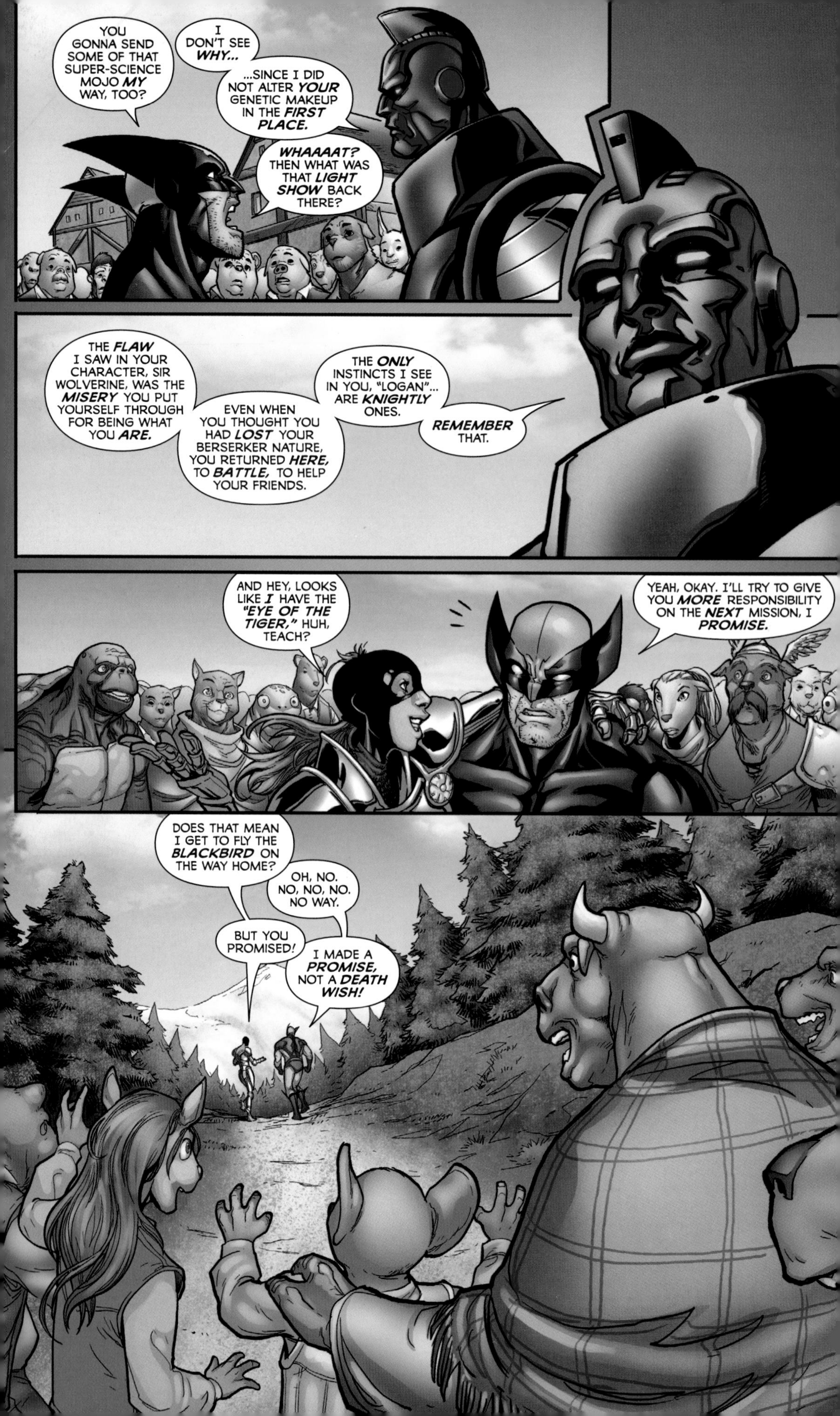
YOU GONNA SEND SOME OF THAT SUPER-SCIENCE MOJO *MY* WAY, TOO?
I DON'T SEE *WHY...*
...SINCE I DID NOT ALTER *YOUR* GENETIC MAKEUP IN THE *FIRST PLACE.*
WHAAAAT? THEN WHAT WAS THAT *LIGHT SHOW* BACK THERE?
THE *FLAW* I SAW IN YOUR CHARACTER, SIR WOLVERINE, WAS THE *MISERY* YOU PUT YOURSELF THROUGH FOR BEING WHAT YOU *ARE.*
EVEN WHEN YOU THOUGHT YOU HAD *LOST* YOUR BERSERKER NATURE, YOU RETURNED *HERE,* TO *BATTLE,* TO HELP YOUR FRIENDS.
THE *ONLY* INSTINCTS I SEE IN YOU, "LOGAN"... ARE *KNIGHTLY* ONES.
REMEMBER THAT.
AND HEY, LOOKS LIKE *I* HAVE THE *"EYE OF THE TIGER,"* HUH, TEACH?
YEAH, OKAY. I'LL TRY TO GIVE YOU *MORE* RESPONSIBILITY ON THE *NEXT* MISSION, I *PROMISE.*
DOES THAT MEAN I GET TO FLY THE *BLACKBIRD* ON THE WAY HOME?
OH, NO. NO, NO, NO. NO WAY.
BUT YOU PROMISED!
I MADE A *PROMISE,* NOT A *DEATH WISH!*

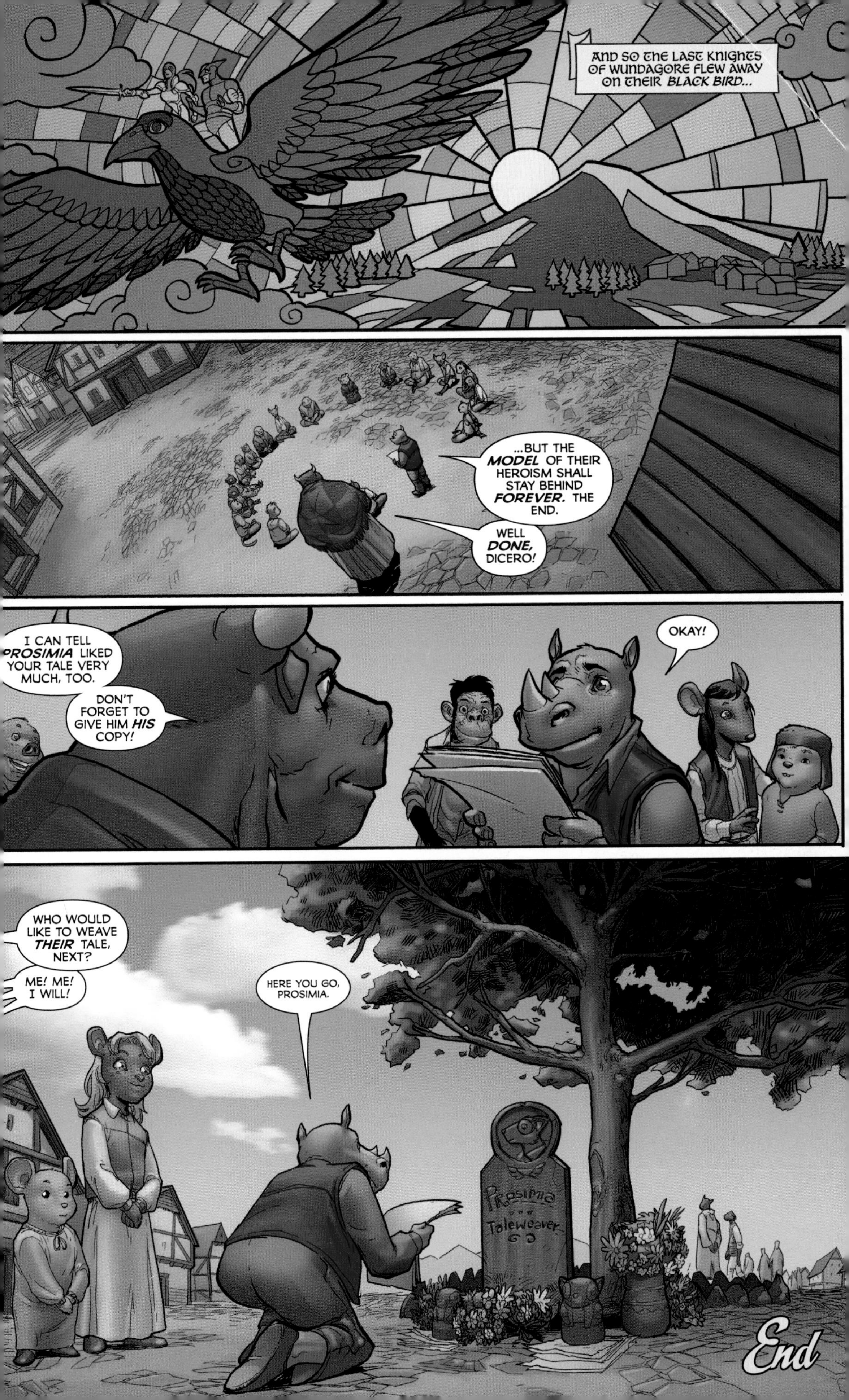
AND SO THE LAST KNIGHTS OF WUNDAGORE FLEW AWAY ON THEIR BLACK BIRD...
...BUT THE MODEL OF THEIR HEROISM SHALL STAY BEHIND FOREVER. THE END.
WELL DONE, DICERO!
I CAN TELL PROSIMIA LIKED YOUR TALE VERY MUCH, TOO.
DON'T FORGET TO GIVE HIM HIS COPY!
OKAY!
WHO WOULD LIKE TO WEAVE THEIR TALE, NEXT?
ME! ME! I WILL!
HERE YOU GO, PROSIMIA.
Prosimia
Taleweaver
End

VISIT US AT
www.abdopublishing.com

Reinforced library bound edition published in 2010 by Spotlight, a division of the ABDO Group, 8000 West 78th Street, Edina, Minnesota 55439. Spotlight produces high-quality reinforced library bound editions for schools and libraries. Published by agreement with Marvel Characters, Inc.

Library of Congress Cataloging-in-Publication Data

Van Lente, Fred.
  The last knights of Wundagore. Part 2 / Fred Van Lente, writer ; Salva Espin, artist ; Ed Dukeshire, letterer. -- Reinforced library bound ed.
      p. cm. -- (Wolverine, first class)
  "Marvel."
  ISBN 978-1-59961-672-8
  1. Graphic novels. 2. Graphic novels. [1. Graphic novels. 2. Superheroes--Fiction.] I. Espin, Salva, ill. II. Dukeshire, Ed. III. Title.
  PZ7.V26Lat 2009
  741.5'973--dc22

                          2009010137

All Spotlight books have reinforced library bindings and
are manufactured in the United States of America.